I0720176

Elena

R.P.G. Colley

Copyright © 2017 Rupert Colley

All rights reserved.
ISBN: 9781739573812

Novels by R.P.G. Colley:

Love and War Series:
The Lost Daughter
The White Venus
Song of Sorrow
The Woman on the Train
The Black Maria
My Brother the Enemy
Anastasia
Elena
The Mist Before Our Eyes
The Darkness We Leave Behind

The Searight Saga:
This Time Tomorrow
The Unforgiving Sea
The Red Oak

The Tales of Little Leaf
Eleven Days in June
Winter in July
Departure in September

**The DI Benedict Paige Crime Series
by JOSHUA BLACK**
And Then She Came Back
The Poison in His Veins
Requiem for a Whistleblower
The Forget-Me-Not Killer
The Canal Boat Killer
A Senseless Killing

https://rupertcolley.com

Elena

Rupertcolley.com

April 1944

Rubble lay all about, clogging up the street; one could smell the charred wood and the evading stench of drains and sewage. An old man with a glass eye led a mule down the street, trying to navigate the beast around the piles of fallen masonry and roof tiles. But to the group of half a dozen or so scruffily dressed children running down the street, overtaking the mule, they'd become so accustomed to such devastation that they hardly noticed it as anything unusual. From the street, they took a left onto Piazza del Plebiscito and stood sheltering from the mid-morning sun within the shadow of the Royal Palace. The American soldiers looked busy today; there were dozens of their jeeps parked haphazardly everywhere, and soldiers running around, some with clipboards, others shouting orders. Elsewhere, clusters of soldiers sat or lay on the stone cobbles, shielding their eyes from the sun, smoking their Camel cigarettes and joking amongst themselves. Shoeshine boys with dirty faces and even dirtier fingers were doing a brisk business. Soldiers, when relaxed, like to have clean boots. Elena and her friends considered their plan of attack. Some of the boys went off to try their luck on these relaxed men with their helmets and big leather boots. *Cioccolato, dolci, per favour?* they'd ask with pitiful voices and grubby, outstretched hands. The soldiers knew the words for chocolates and sweets by now and they also knew if they wanted to be spared the cloying attention of these street urchins, it was usually best to give them something, however small, and be rid of them. Elena would have joined them, she usually did, she was part of the gang, but her attention had been taken by a group of soldiers, equally redolent, to her right, lounging on some stone steps beneath an archway. They seemed very separate from their fellow soldiers, and she couldn't work out whether it was by choice or not. She'd never seen such men before – they were all black. She crept towards them, keeping to the wall, not wanting to be seen. One rattled off a tune on his mouth organ, two others, lying on the steps, were having an arm wrestle. If she could scrounge some chocolate off these Negros, she thought, it would elevate her position within the group.

One of the soldiers, a huge man with square shoulders and long legs, his helmet pushed back, strolled languidly towards the fountain. He pushed a brass button and water spurted from the mouth of a dolphin pouring into a shell-shaped tub beneath it. Elena watched as he bent his head and took in mouthfuls of water. She crept up behind him. She watched him as he rolled up his sleeves, removed his watch and put it in the side pocket of his tunic. She felt a ripple of excitement wash over her – now, that'd be something. Imagine the kudos she'd get from the others if she could snatch the watch. But no, it could be worth a lot and the bigger boys would take it for themselves. Better to take it home to her sister. Nina could sell it. They'd live like queens. It was worth the risk – as a girl it was easier. The boys risked too much of a beating but as a girl… She glanced back at the other soldiers. Their attention had been diverted by a pretty woman passing by, wearing a black dress, swinging her hips and swinging a wicker basket. A couple of them whistled at her. Elena crept closer and closer still to the point she could almost tap the soldier on the back. Cupping his gigantic hands, he splashed his face with water, letting out a groan of satisfaction. Quickly, she reached out and fished the watch out of his pocket. She turned to walk away, trying her best not to run and arouse suspicion – just a girl walking by. 'Hey…' he shouted in a booming voice. She turned, saw the quizzical look on his face, and then, catching her eye, the sudden realisation. 'Hey, you…' She ran.

She ran as fast as possible, confident that she'd soon escape him. She heard the other soldiers laughing at their colleague running after the little street girl. Part of her was enjoying this. She headed for a side street, off the square, and ran straight into the woman with the black dress. Apologising, she turned to see the soldier was almost upon her. With a yelp, she made off. She heard him shouting, 'You, hey you. Stop! My watch, give me back my damned watch.'

She headed north along Via Toledo, then took the next left, onto Via Carlo de Cesare, a steep, narrow street. Laundry, like white flags, hanging from balconies. Then the second right – heading for home. Yet, he was still there, she could hear his heavy army boots pounding the rutted pavement and cobblestones right behind her. She wasn't enjoying this any more, chased by a huge man, black as the night with hands the size of bats. She was almost home. She should avoid it; he'd know where she lived, there'd be no escape. But she didn't know where else to go; she was frightened. She'd go home and Nina would protect her, Nina would know what to do.

Climbing over a pile of bricks and stone, Elena stumbled into her house, squeezing through the gap where the front door hung off its hinges, and straight into the living room-cum-kitchen. She found Nina sitting at the table darning a pair of stockings, drawings of children and donkeys scattered across the table.

'What's the matter?'

'There's a…' Elena tried to catch her breath. 'A giant…'

And then he was there, pushing at the door to squeeze through. Elena stepped back towards her sister.

'Right then, you little scamp,' said the soldier, having pushed his way in. His eyes darted from one girl to the other, his chest heaving from running in the heat of the day. Elena had never seen a man so big, his black skin shone with perspiration, he wiped his almost invisible pencil moustache. He put his hand out, palm up. 'My watch, please.' He repeated the phrase in Italian. *'Il mio orologio, per favour.'*

'You… you speak Italian?' asked Nina slowly.

'Sure I do, one hundred per cent,' he said in Italian in his deep voice that seemed to shake the ground. 'And your… your…' He pointed at Elena.

'Sister,' said Elena. 'I'm her sister.'

'Right,' he said. 'So, come on… my watch, if you don't mind.'

Gingerly, Elena stepped forward and handed the soldier back his watch, placing it in his huge, upturned hand. He looked at it, turning it over, as if making sure it was still intact, listening to its tick. 'Thank you,' he said, reattaching it to his wrist.

'You stole that?' whispered Nina.

'Yes, she did; *she* stole that,' said the soldier. He looked around, his nose twitching with the smell of mould and general decay. 'One hell of a place you've got here. So, where are your parents? I'd like to have a word with them.'

'They're dead,' said Elena firmly.

He raised an eyebrow. 'Dead? Both of them?'

'Yes. And Aunt Luisa. She's dead too.'

'Oh. OK, then,'

'August last year,' said Nina. 'The bombing.'

'Lordy, I'm sorry to hear that. Anyone else here apart from you two?'

'No,' said Elena.

'Our brother was taken by the Germans to work in Germany,' said Nina.

'I see now. So it's just the two of you, right?'

'Yes.'

He started to wander around the room, taking in their little apartment which, like any other building in Naples in 1944, looked shattered. The wallpaper mouldy, the paint on the windowsills flaking off, brown, sticky tape on the cracks across the windows, a picture of the Madonna with child now layered in dust, dead flies stuck to the flypaper, the brown-stained kitchen sink, the cracked tiles, the rust-coloured taps. He picked up a little figurine of Christ, ran his finger along the spines of a few, dusty old books that had belonged to their father, opened the door to the toilet, quickly closing it again. The two girls watched him, occasionally glancing at each other, wondering what was going through his mind. He seemed to fill the space of their tiny apartment, like watching a giant in a doll's house. He carried with him an air of propriety without appearing aggressive, assertive without being threatening, confident without being patronising.

'How do you make your money? Apart from stealing, that is,' he added, looking at Elena sideways.

Elena looked down.

'I darn socks and mend things,' said Nina. 'But one day I'm going to write a book, and draw it too.'

'These pictures?' he asked, motioning at the drawings on the table. 'The donkey?'

'Yes.'

'They're good. Very good.'

'Tell him what Signore Battistini said,' said Elena.

'No.'

'What did this Signore Battistini say?'

Elena knew Nina would be cross, but in her excitement wanting to say something shocking, she ploughed on regardless. 'Signore Battistini reckons Nina should take her clothes off for you soldiers—'

'Elena! Shut up.'

'Signore Battistini says she could earn loads.'

'Does he indeed?'

'I'm not going to,' said Nina, crossing her arms over her chest.

'And so you shouldn't. How old are you?' he asked both of them.

Nina was fifteen; Elena twelve.

'So you're Elena and you are Nina. Nice to meet you. I'm Brad.'

'You're one of our liberators,' said Nina.

'Glad you think so.'

'Would you like some coffee?' asked Elena for no other reason than it sounded grown-up.

'You have coffee?'

'No.'

He laughed. 'Thank you for the offer, anyhow, Missy.' He checked the time on his watch. 'Lordy, I'd better be off.'

He paused at the door. 'It's been…' He looked at them both, these young orphan girls with their black hair and their dusty faces and wide eyes, eyes that should have been innocent but had been toughened by war and necessity.

'Would you like to come back one day?' asked Elena, feeling that perhaps she should have asked her sister before blurting out such an invitation.

'That's kind of you, Miss, one hundred per cent, but as much as I'd like to, I cannot. You see, we're heading north this very night. We've got some Germans to catch up with and some fighting to do. There's still a long way to go in this war. Naples is one hell of a city. One day, when it's over and I'm a rich man, I'm gonna come back and find myself a pretty Italian wife. So I'll say goodbye now.'

'It's been nice meeting you,' said Elena, conscious of how small her voice sounded next to this enormous American with his black, shiny skin.

He hesitated, his hand on the side of the door. His eyes seemed to melt for a moment. Removing his watch from his wrist, he offered it to Elena. 'Here,' he said, 'you can have it…'

Elena hesitated, fearing a trick of some sort.

'Go on, take it. You can probably sell it.'

Elena glanced at her sister for approval, then, like a nervous cat taking food from the hand of a stranger, reached out and took the watch. 'T-thank you,' she spluttered.

'And for you,' he said to Nina. 'Here…' He passed her a few bank notes. 'Buy yourself some bread if you can. Feed yourselves up for a day or two.'

The sisters simply stared at him, still expecting to do something in return. Elena thought of Signore Battistini and his furtive manner. But no, the American winked at her, said he had to go, and left.

The girls looked at the space he'd just occupied, wondering whether this vision of kindness had just been that – a vision.

Eventually, Nina broke their spellbound silence. 'Look at all this money. My God. Mary, Mother of Jesus, we thank thee. He liked my drawings too. Here, let's see that watch.'

It had a black leather strap, a black face with white numbers, hands the shape of swords showing the right time, and a little circle at the bottom for the seconds hand. The glass was cracked right through the middle from the twelve down to the seven. 'I guess it must be American,' said Elena, mesmerised by the idea she was holding something that had come from so far away. She loved it.

'My God,' said Nina, 'that could be worth a fortune.'

'What do you mean?'

'We'll sell it and—'

'No,' screeched Elena. 'We're not selling this.'

'Why not, think—'

'No, he gave it to me,' she shouted, backing away from her, clasping the watch behind her back. 'He gave it to me! Brad gave it to *me*. A gift. I'm never giving this away. Not for all the money in the world. He gave it to me and if you ever touch it, I'll…'

'OK, Elena, all right. I won't sell it.'

'I don't want you to even touch it. You promise?'

Nina sighed heavily. 'If that's what you want then yes, OK, I promise.'

But Elena didn't believe her. She'd wear it, she thought, even if it was too big, and she'd never let it out of her sight. Not for a single second. 'I want to keep it,' she said, almost to herself. 'And one day, he'll come back.'

'No, he won't.'

'He said he would,' she snapped.

'And you're going to be his *pretty Italian wife*, are you?'

Elena decided not to deign her sister's sarcasm with an answer.

June 1955

Nina loved driving around too fast on her Vespa. It annoyed the men; girls shouldn't be seen on mopeds wearing helmets – it was undignified. And Elena loved riding pillion, feeling the wind rush through her hair as they skirted around the city. But today she was feeling sad – because today her sister was leaving her.

'Elena, it's not that bad,' said Nina, once she'd parked up the Vespa. 'It's only for two nights. I'll be back on Monday afternoon.'

Elena almost stomped her feet. 'But why,' she moaned. 'I don't understand.'

They were in the car park at the back of their apartment block, the asphalt soft, almost melting, in the mid-morning heat. Beyond the car park, a group of boys played basketball, a couple still managing to smoke at the same time.

Nina put her hands on Elena's shoulders and leant her head towards her, the way she often did when she had something important to say. It meant Elena had to concentrate on what she was saying. 'You've done it before, Elena, and you were fine. It's good for you to cope on your own every–'

'Doesn't mean I have to like it.'

Nina hugged her sister. 'You'll be fine. You've got food in the fridge, you got Signora da Sangallo next door and you can always phone me. Yeah? Anytime, you can give me a ring. Before you know it, it'll be Monday and I'll be back, and you'll say "I love it by myself". Just like you did last time, remember?'

'Suppose.'

'So, you're going swimming now, yes?'

'I just need to get my stuff.'

'Good. Don't forget your purse and–'

'And don't forget my keys; yes, I know. They're here,' she said, patting her handbag.

'Good girl. Come on; give me another hug.'

Elena could see that her sister was more upset than she was; it was always the case. Nina thought her incapable of looking after herself. But she was 23 now; perfectly competent. She stepped back and watched as Nina put on her helmet, as if she was a gladiator about to go into the ring, got on the moped and switched on its high-pitched engine. 'Have fun,' Elena shouted.

'I will. Look after yourself now.' And with that, Nina cruised down the short driveway that bordered their block of flats. Indicating right, she paused at the metal gates, looked left and right and was off. Elena gave her a final wave goodbye.

Back in the apartment, Elena poured herself a glass of lemonade and sat on the balcony which, at this time of day, was always in the shade. She watched the boys playing their basketball, whooping and shouting at each other, the thud of the ball bouncing continually on the tarmac. The sisters lived in this second-floor, two-bedroom rented apartment not too far from the city centre. They'd moved in last winter, the winter of 1954. Elena had worried about moving out of their old apartment – what would happen if Brad came back, looking for her? She left her new address with the new occupant, insisting that she promised to pass it on if any black Americans came looking for her. Nina and Elena were alone in the world now. It wasn't always the case. Once, there were six of them – all crowded into a tiny flat in the shanty backstreets just behind the Piazza del Plebiscito – two parents, two sisters, a brother and an elderly aunt. One by one, all of them had died – all but Elena and Nina. Their parents and Aunt Luisa had died in the huge bombing raid in August 1943, and Paolo, their brother, had been rounded up by the Germans and sent to Germany to work as a forced labourer. He never came back. Five years later, they received a letter, saying he'd died of disease and malnutrition. So now they lived in this lovely apartment, just the two of them, paid out of

Nina's royalties. And how lovely it was; such a far cry from before. They had a bedroom each. This in itself was a revelation and a luxury – before she had to share with both her sister and Aunt Luisa, a dreadful, bad-tempered woman who spent most of the night farting in her sleep. Nina often used to say, 'Imagine if Papa could see us now? He'd think we'd become millionaires.' They had carpets of red in their living room, as red as a plum tomato. They had striped wallpaper coloured various shades of gold and a clock on the wall in the shape of a guitar. They had a standard lamp and in the kitchen a refrigerator. Nina often joked, 'Mama wouldn't have known what a refrigerator was even if she bumped into one.' The years of poverty were behind them. Nina had written a book, a children's story about a neglected donkey and a boy who saves it. Her friends loved it; told her to send it to a publisher. Eventually, she did. And the publisher loved it and showered her with love. And then all of Italy loved it. It got translated into dozens of languages. A simple story, a fable, with simple pictures, and it made Nina rich! The only blot on Elena's horizon was Roberto, Nina's new boyfriend. He was a nice enough man, certainly good-looking with his natty suits and sunglasses, looking like some model out of one of those fashion magazines that Nina liked so much, but their developing relationship was a cause of concern for her. They seemed to be in love, and this was not good news. What if they got married? Nina had already promised that, whatever happened, Elena would always be able to live with Nina. But Roberto would have a say, wouldn't he? And he might not like the idea of having to live with his wife's simple sister.

But that was for another day. Right now, having finished her lemonade, it was time to go to the pool. She grabbed her satchel. Everything she needed was already prepared – her swimming suit, cap, towel and goggles. Elena was a good swimmer; at least that's what everyone said. It was the one thing she could do. Breaststroke, backstroke, front crawl – she could do the lot. Nina called her the female Johnny Weissmuller, to which she would always reply with Weissmuller's famous Tarzan cry. The outdoor pool, just a ten-minute walk from home, was meant to be the largest in the city. The staff there knew her by name and often asked whether she'd broken any world records lately. There was a boy who worked there as a lifeguard, Antonio, who she suspected liked her. He had the torso of a god but, flattered though she was, it meant nothing to Elena. She had the love of her life and Antonio could flex his biceps and thrust out his chest as much as he liked, it wasn't going to change her mind. She had her man. He just didn't know it yet.

Finished with her swimming, Elena decided to venture into town. There was a café there she'd been to with Nina and she wanted to go again. Why not, she thought. She was alone, she had a bit of money, she could do as she pleased. It was but a ten-minute bus ride away. But it took a little longer than usual – it was late afternoon, the roads were clogged with rush hour traffic. Alighting from the bus, she had a little difficulty finding it. But there it was – in a small square with its own church, opposite a park dense with palm trees – Café Italiano with its blue and white striped awning. Inside was a shrine to Italian football – framed pictures and portraits of Italian greats past and present – Sandro Mazzola, Silvio Piola, Giuseppe Meazza and several others. But today Elena decided to sit outside. She ordered a coffee and a slice of chocolate cake, and, enjoying the sun, sat there feeling content with life watching the world rushing by. Looking through her satchel, she realised she'd forgotten her swimming cap at the pool. No matter. Nearby, a beggar strummed his guitar singing folk songs that told of heartache and lost love.

At first, Elena took little notice of the man's reedy voice, just vaguely aware of someone speaking English too loudly in what sounded like an American accent. 'This seems a nice enough place, Minnie,' he said. 'What would you prefer, honey – inside or out?'

'Inside. I'm so hot.' Elena noticed the overweight black woman in a sheer white dress.

She heard the man speak to the waiter in Italian. He seemed fluent with his strange accent but still, she took little notice of the man in a pale, linen suit, listening instead to the singer's plaintive cry for a girl called Maria. She took a sip of coffee. It was then, at the moment her coffee cup was touching her lips, she heard the American say in Italian, 'You've got one hell of a place here.'

The world stopped for a moment. The man and his woman disappeared inside. 'You've got one hell of a place here.' She'd never forget those words, those exact words, in that voice, that same voice, that accent. The hot liquid seared through the thin cotton of her skirt, piercing the skin on her thigh. With a yelp, she shot to her feet, using her napkin to wipe away the spilt coffee. The waiter darted over. 'You OK, Miss?'

'Yes, what? Yes, I'm fine, it's nothing.' Gingerly, she sat back down and placed the cup back on its saucer, her mind whirling. The man was gone, just the waiter with a white cloth looped over his arm looming over her with a slightly condescending smile.

'*Maria, Maria, you broke my heart into a million pieces…*'

'Did… did that man stay?'

'What man? The American. Yes, Miss, he went inside with his wife.'

'His wife? Oh. Thank you.'

He bowed, heard someone calling out for him and left.

She placed her hand against her chest and felt the thudding of her heart. That phrase, 'one hell of a place here'. Was it really him, after all these years? All she had to do was to walk into the café and see for herself. But it was too much. She'd waited for this for eleven years, dreamt of this moment, fantasised about it a thousand times or more. Dreams didn't come true; not in the real world. It was all too much for her. *'Maria, whatever happened to our love? Cast aside like an old discarded toy; oh, Maria, Maria, my love…'*

'One hell of a place here, one hell of a place'. As if in a trance, Elena slowly rose to her feet, wiped at the still-warm stain of coffee on her skirt and swallowed. Her mind blank, she stepped into the inside of the café, her eyes squinting against the darkened interior, just a couple of light bulbs, breathing in the aroma of fresh coffee, the whiff of cinnamon. Blinking away the darkness, she saw the outline of two figures at a table. A waiter rushed by, whistling, balancing a tray on his fingertips. The faces of the footballers seemed to be watching her with their wide, smiling eyes and white teeth. One foot in front of the other, she approached, a thumping in her chest she hadn't experienced since the dark days. Yes, she thought, her breaths coming in short, almost panicked bursts, it was him. The intervening decade had hardly left a mark – his skin, just as smooth, the light reflecting off its blackness, his wide, affectionate eyes that, when they held you within their gaze, made you feel as if nothing else mattered in his world, his moustache still the same, that determined jaw. 'It's this heat, I'm just not hungry,' she heard the woman say in her irritating, high-pitched tone.

'I'll get us some water, honey.'

She stopped at the table. 'Excuse me,' he said in Italian. 'Can I also get a glass… oh, I'm sorry, ma'am, I thought you–
'

'Hello, Brad,' she said tonelessly despite her leaping heart.

He narrowed his eyes. 'Do I know you?' His voice was as deep as she remembered it, exuding such strength, such confidence.

'Yes, you know me,' she said, aware that her own voice sounded so brittle and far away. 'You… you said you'd come back one day and…' She tried to smile. 'Now you have.'

'Who is this?' she heard the woman say.

'Hell if I know, hun.'

His words, spoken in English, cut her. This wasn't how she imagined it would be. But then her dreams had never accounted for the presence of a woman.

'You remember me,' she said. 'You must…' She saw the confused expression in those wide eyes of his, his head tilted to one side. 'Don't you remember me?'

Slowly, he shook his head. 'I'm sorry, Miss, but I think you got me mistook for some other guy,' he said, his voice laced with sympathy while, next to him, she felt the eyes of his wife bore into her.

'I…' She didn't know what to say; she hadn't planned for this scenario. 'I'm sorry.' She turned and fled, their conversation in her ears, 'Who *was* that?' 'I don't know, hun.' 'Well, she sure knows you.' She paused at her table outside, fished out some change from her purse and left it on the table, much of it tumbling to the ground in her haste to escape. The guitarist had set up outside a rival café further down the street, his longing for Maria still audible above the heavy drone of traffic. Hurrying across the road, she sat on the low wall that bordered the park, catching her breath in a spot shaded by a palm tree. People passed by, a beggar asked for money and someone asked her the time at the same point the church clock struck five. She looked at none of them, spoke to none of them, keeping her eyes fixed on the Café Italiano, waiting, her heart refusing to calm down. She knew she'd wait all night if need be. As it was, she waited a little more than half an hour when she saw them emerge from the inside of the café. He was as tall as she remembered, towering over his fat wife in her painfully white dress. She watched as he took her arm, placed a trilby on his head, and together left the café, heading northwards. Elena slid off the wall, waited for the traffic to pass, and ran back across towards the café. She waited for a few moments and saw them turn right into Via Concordia, and made off to follow them. A voice in her head told her she was being silly, the tension biting into her heart told her likewise, but, she concluded, she had no option. The opportunity would never come again. She had to do it. And so, for the next ten or twelve minutes, she followed the American couple walking on the shaded side of the street, holding hands, strolling, as holidaymakers do in hot cities, taking in their surroundings, pointing things out to each other. Elena followed some twenty yards behind, not daring to take her eyes off them for a second, fearful they should disappear in the blink of an eye. They seemed to be heading for Piazzetta Cariati, she thought, and they seemed to know where they were. Not once did they stop to consult a map or ask anyone for directions. Sure enough, a final left turn and they were on Piazzetta Cariati. Elena knew there were several hotels here and she had to run to try to catch up before they disappeared into one. She panicked a moment when, looking left and right; they were nowhere to be seen. Then she saw them, heading across the square, disturbing a brood of pigeons along the way. They cut through a children's game of football. A stray ball came Brad's way. He trapped it beneath his foot and, with the side of his shoe, passed it back. 'He's Pele,' shouted one of the boys. Brad bowed, sweeping the air with his hat, accepting the applause. Hovering behind a tree in the middle of the square, Elena watched as they approached the Schilizzi hotel. The building, three or four stories tall, was constructed with pale stucco walls, with shutters on the windows painted a faded green, and simple wrought-iron balconies jutted out from the upper floors. A doorman appeared from within the shadows and with smiles all around, opened the one side of the glass door for his distinguished American guests. So, thought Elena, at least she knew where they were staying. By the time they checked out, the woman would be going home by herself, and he, Brad, would be hers once more, and she'd be his pretty Italian wife. Just as she'd always wished for.

*

As soon as she was home, Elena rang her sister. A man answered. She soon worked out it was Roberto's father. No, he said, Nina and his son had gone out for the evening. No, he didn't know what time they'd be back. Did she want to leave a message? 'No, thank you, *signore*.' She put the phone down. Then, immediately rang back. The man picked up again, the annoyance clear in his voice. Elena apologised. 'I've changed my mind, *signore*. I'd like to leave a message after all.'

A pause. 'Well, go on then, what is it?'

'Yes, erm, could you tell Nina… No, erm, perhaps, no, that's not right…'

'Young lady, I give you five seconds.'

'What? Oh yes, erm… tell her… tell her, yes, could you tell her please… he's back.'

'He's back?'

'Yes.'

'And that's it – he's back.'

'Yes, thank you, *signore.*'

She hoped she would never have to speak to him again. She turned the radio on in the living room. Cab Calloway was playing. Dancing now, she'd never felt so excited. If only she'd been able to speak to Nina. Nina would have told her what to do. She needed to eat. Quickly, she boiled some plain pasta and, adding a couple of tomatoes and a sprinkling of basil, ate quickly. She showered, singing, then spent some time in her bedroom, the door open, the radio coming through from the living room, deciding what to wear. It had to be right. She loved her bedroom – purple walls plastered with photos of Hollywood stars ripped out of magazines, a white dresser and a large, oval-shaped mirror. She tried on various dresses and shirts with increasing agitation – none pleased her. They made her look too clumsy, too provincial somehow. Old-fashioned. She tried to think what sort of outfit Nina would wear. She'd borrow one of her dresses but Nina was a whole size bigger. Time was passing. She went to the kitchen, had another glass of lemonade, and tried to calm down. Stealing into her sister's bedroom, she borrowed one of Nina's bras – they were the same cup size, but Nina's were more uplift. Eventually, she decided on the first outfit she tried – a pink skirt, the colour of cotton candy, and a light green top that crossed over her bosom. A necklace of black beads finished it off. She took some of Nina's perfume, deciding that her own perfume might come across as a bit 'young'. She applied a layer of mascara and took a while deciding on which lipstick to wear. While there, she borrowed Nina's fan, a souvenir from a recent trip to the opera to see Madame Butterfly. She twirled around in front of her sister's full-length mirror – yes, she thought with much relief, she looked the part. She was ready, as ready as she'd ever be. There was just the one thing to remember, the most important thing of all – Brad's watch. She'd always kept it in a small leather case on her dresser. Sitting on her bed, she took time to admire it once again as she'd done many, many times over the years. It still worked – showing the correct time. It still had its original black leather strap, and hands the shape of swords upon the black face, and a little circle at the bottom for the seconds hand. It still had the crack. Nina had suggested getting it repaired but no, somehow the crack was part of it, part of its identity. She'd loved the watch the moment she set eyes on it – it seemed to promise so much, a life far away from war-torn Naples, far away from a life without clean water and decent food. And now, eleven years later, she would return it to the man who had given it to her. So, she thought, time to go back to the hotel. At the apartment door, handbag over her shoulder, key in hand, she had her first wave of doubt. After all, this was the moment she'd been waiting for since 1944; she was on the cusp of something new. These moments don't come often. Then there was the fact that she wasn't accustomed to dressing up. With this in mind, she grabbed a thin, long coat from the hatstand. Thus, attired, Elena went out to claim her destiny.

Feeling self-conscious, her eyes down, Elena stepped into the bar of Hotel Schilizzi. The small seating area included a few armchairs upholstered in floral fabric and a low coffee table stacked with old magazines. A ceiling fan whirred overhead. The lighting was warm but dim, with frosted glass sconces lining the walls. The scent of strong coffee and a hint of lemon polish lingered in the air. The large octagon-shaped clock showed eight o'clock.

Trying to muster a degree of confidence, she approached the bar and smiled at the barman, a man with slicked-back black hair, streaked with grey, and a neatly trimmed moustache. Elena ordered a Coca-Cola with lemon and ice. The man asked whether she was staying at the hotel and Elena flushed as she confessed she was meeting a friend. Taking her drink, Elena chose her armchair carefully, pushing it slightly away from the potted yucca plant in order to keep an eye on reception. Fanning herself with her sister's fan, she watched people come and go, and tried rehearsing what she was going to say to him but each time she placed herself within the scenario, she felt so crippled with nerves, she couldn't do it. Instead, she stroked Brad's watch and told herself she'd be OK, that Brad would take the situation in hand.

Time passed. An hour, then another. She'd got herself another coke, which she sipped slowly through a straw and cursed when she needed to have a pee. She couldn't risk leaving her spot in case…. She held on until she could hold on no longer. As quick as she could, she dashed to the loo and back. She felt a little dizzy. Taking another sip of drink, now not as cold as it had been, she forced herself to calm down, to take deep breaths. And that was the exact moment she heard his voice. A stab, like that of a knife, drove into her heart. She turned and saw him, his back to her, leaning on the bar. 'Yes, ice would be good,' he was saying to the bartender in Italian. He was wearing a pinstripe brown suit with brown, very shiny leather shoes. As if aware of Elena's eyes boring into his back, he turned, a drink in his hand. He screwed up his eyes, then, recognising her, stepped towards her.

'Hello there,' he said in his deep voice, a skewered smile on his lips.

Elena stumbled to her feet. 'Hello,' she said, offering her trembling hand. He took it.

He took a sip of his drink. 'A nightcap,' he said, raising his glass. 'You're the girl in the café, aren't you?'

'Yes, I am,' she replied, conscious of how shaky her voice sounded.

'But...' He tilted his head to one side as if better to understand. 'How come... How did you know? Is this just a coincidence or...?'

'I just wanted to say hello.'

He considered her for a few moments, realising that the girl must have followed him. 'Oh. Right. OK. Well, we've said hello now...' He made as if to go. 'So if you'll excuse–'

'Don't you remember me?'

He paused, scrutinising Elena's face. 'I can't recall... no, hang on a minute, oh my good Lord...'

Elena grinned.

'Lordy, Lord, it's *you*...' He leaned forward again as if to see her better. 'Well I never.'

'You said you'd come back.'

'Did I? I guess I must've.' Taking the armchair opposite her, he said, 'Wow, that sure was a while ago. What was your name?'

Her name had slipped his memory. Sitting down also, she tried not to show her disappointment. 'Elena.'

'Elena. Elena… Yes, I remember now. Elena. Hell, yes.' He sat back in the chair, crossing his legs. 'Hey, do you want a drink?'

'No, I'm fine, thank you.' She slurped at her drink as if to emphasise the point. 'I like your shoes.'

He glanced down at them – as if he'd forgotten what they looked like. 'Well, thank you. So, Elena…' He said her name slowly, elongating each syllable. 'How have you been doing these last… these last ten years?'

'Eleven years.'

'Eleven.'

I've thought of you every day, every night, since the day you left. I've dreamt of you, dreamed that you'd come back and tell me you've thought of me just as much and that you'd missed me, and that you'll take me back to America and look after me and hold me in your arms. And there's a very nice boy at the swimming pool, Antonio, and my sister reckons he likes me but I don't care; I've never wanted a boyfriend because, in my mind, in my dreams, I had you, always you. Instead, she merely said she was fine, that she liked swimming and she liked the Tarzan films with Johnny Weissmuller and that she lived with her sister. He laughed out loud, a huge loud laugh. 'Do you remember her?' she asked, her fingers gripping her glass.

'Who? Your sister?' He shook his head. 'Can't say I do.' Seeing the crestfallen expression on her face, he apologised.

'Do you… do you still live in America?' she asked.

'Oh yeah, ma'am, I sure do. One hundred per cent. Me and my wife live in New Jersey. Have you heard of New Jersey? It sure is a big, big city. But it ain't Naples. Nowhere is like Naples. In Naples, no one calls me nigger.'

'So why don't you move here?' she asked, trying to contain herself.

'No, Missy. See, I got my own business back home and it's doing great. I sell jukeboxes.'

'What's that?'

He explained. 'I have a partner, a white guy called Tony. So white I've seen ghosts with more colour on them. Tony sells to the white folk, 'cos there's no way they're buying from a Negro, and I sell to the black 'cos they don't want white folk's goods. Ain't it all silly? Between us, me and Tony do just fine. Anyway, my wife, she's called Minnie, she wouldn't want to leave New Jersey. She's expecting, you know.'

'Expecting what?'

He laughed again, that laugh that seemed to move the furniture. 'Why, a baby, of course.'

The shattering of glass made them both jump, the glass of coke slipping from her clasp and breaking on the wooden flooring. 'A baby?'

'Your glass – are you alright, Miss?'

A waiter, unable to disguise his annoyance, appeared with a dustpan and brush. 'No matter, no matter,' he said, sweeping up the fragments of glass. 'Can I get you another drink, Miss?'

'A baby?' So Brad's wife was pregnant, not fat.

'Yes, siree! A baby, baby, baby. My old ma reckons it's gonna be a li'l girl. Says it's all to do with the shape of–'

'I've got your watch.' She hadn't meant to play her trump card so abruptly but she couldn't bear to hear another word about the stupid baby.

The waiter, satisfied he'd cleared the worst of it, bowed and made his exit.

'My what? What watch?'

Had he forgotten that as well? She'd played this conversation so many times over the years. She'd planned every word, every gesture. She had her part; he had his. But none of it was going according to plan. It was as if he was reading a different play and she had no idea how to bring it round. 'Your watch,' she said. 'Don't you remember? You gave me your watch.' Reaching inside her handbag, she pulled out the leather case. 'Here,' she said, passing it to him.

He flicked open the latch. His eyebrows shot up on seeing it. 'Oh, my good Lord. Did I give you this?'

'Yes, of course you did?' she asked, a prick of tears behind her eyes. 'Don't you remember *anything*?' She hadn't meant for it to come out so harshly but she couldn't help it – a harshness borne out of desperation.

Catching her tone, he looked at her. Something – a sort of realisation, seemed to fall on his features. 'Oh my… I think I see what's going on here.' Placing the case on the little table, next to his glass, he leant forward, clasping his hands. 'Elena, you followed me here from the café, didn't you?'

A wave of shame swept over her as almost imperceptibly she nodded her head.

He smiled a smile laced with sympathy. But she didn't want his sympathy, anything but that. 'I'm sorry,' she whispered.

'No matter. You're a good girl, I can see that. But listen, what happened back then, back during the war, it affected all of us in different ways. I don't know about you but I still get nightmares. You understand – you were there. You suffered too, I know that. I saw it for myself. But we're in 1955 now, Elena. Ten years. We have to move on, you know.'

'Eleven years.' Putting her face in her hands, she let the tears come. She hadn't wanted to – to cry – but now she'd started, she couldn't stem the flow. Between sobs, she gasped, 'I don't want to; I don't want to move on.'

She felt his arm around her shoulder. He'd moved out of his chair and was now crouching next to hers. He passed her a pristine white handkerchief. 'Come on now, Miss. Life don't stand still, you know. You have to move with it. You're still young, you've still gotta whole lot of living to do. You can't get hung up about some old negro who lives on the other side of the world. Even if he does have a fine-lookin' pair of shoes.'

Despite herself, she laughed; a laugh mixed in with the tears.

'That's more like it. That's what this miserable world needs – more laughing.'

She blew her nose in his handkerchief. Through her tears, Elena saw a pair of women's shoes in front of her, black and shiny, such elegance.

'Brad, what the heck?'

Brad, standing, his knees creaking, said, 'Honey…'

'I wondered what the heck happened to you.'

'Honey, let me introduce you to a brave young lady. This is Elena. Elena, this is my good wife, Minnie.'

The woman, holding her hands beneath her belly, tried to smile but couldn't disguise the doubt in her eyes. 'Delighted, I'm sure,' she said.

Elena caught Brad putting a finger on his lips, shushing his wife. Crouching down again, he placed his hand on Elena's shoulder. 'So now, this is what we're going to do, OK? We're gonna put you in a cab to take you home to your sister. Hell, she must be fretting about you right now. I'll pay–'

'It's OK, I can–'

'Miss, it'd be a privilege, now. And I want you to get a good night's sleep and tomorrow...' He looked up at his wife. 'Tomorrow is a new day, Miss. The first of many. How old are you, Elena?'

'Twenty-three.'

'Twenty-three? Is that all? You've still got all your tomorrows ahead of you, girl. Think of that. Listen, I want you to promise me something... Elena, tomorrow you must start living for yourself. You understand me?' Reassured by the touch of his hand on her shoulder, she tried to say yes. 'The war's finished now, and your war is finished. You've got to live your life now. No looking back. Yeah? You promise me now?'

She nodded.

'No, come on, you can do better than that.'

'Yes,' she whispered, gripping Brad's handkerchief. 'I promise. One hundred per cent.'

'What have you got ahead of you?'

'All my tomorrows.'

'That's right. Good girl. Hey, hun,' he said to Minnie. 'Can you get reception to call a cab for this young lady?' Turning to Elena, he asked for her address. 'Hang on, let me jot that down.'

'I can remember that,' said Minnie.

'Yeah, but I might not.'

They watched as Minnie went to reception. 'Do you want your watch back?' asked Elena.

'Sure thing,' he said, not noticing the disappointment flash across Elena's face. 'I never thought I'd see that again. I wore that every day of combat.'

'Until I stole it off you.'

'No, Miss, let's say until the day I gave it to you.'

Elena swallowed. She placed her hand on her heart, willing it to slow down. 'When's the baby due?'

'Doctors say November some time.'

'Do you want a boy or a girl?'

Brad stroked his chin. 'Honest to God, I don't mind. Long as it's born healthy, one hundred per cent, that's all I'm caring about.'

Minnie returned. 'Two minutes,' she said.

Brad struggled up to his feet, muttering, 'These knees ain't getting any younger.' Taking his place next to his wife, he said, 'I was just telling Elena here our good news.'

Minnie patted her belly. 'It sure is.'

'Congratulations, Madam.'

'Well, thank you, darling. Your name Elena?'

'Yes. Elena.'

'That's such a pretty name, ain't it, Brad?'

He winked. 'It sure is, hun; a beautiful name.'

*

Half an hour later, Elena was back at home. Collapsing on her bed, her mind still whirling, she lay on her back looking at the ceiling where she'd put a poster of Sophia Loren. How beautiful she is, she thought, with those luscious lips, those bedazzling eyes. If only she could be as beautiful as Sophia. As she'd left, both Brad and Minnie had hugged her. 'Remember,' he'd said, 'you have all your tomorrows ahead of you. Live them to the full, you got me?'

All my tomorrows. The tears rolled down her cheeks onto the pillow. If only I was as beautiful as Sophia Loren; she'd never lose her man. No man would ever turn his back on Sophia Loren.

Still dressed, she was almost asleep, her pillow still damp, the tears dried on her cheek when the telephone rang shrilly from the living room. Groaning, Elena stumbled through. The guitar-shaped clock showed a few minutes past midnight.

'Elena! Thank God. Where have you *been*?'

Leaning against the wall, Elena simply replied, 'Out.'

'Out? Is that it? But where were you? I've been ringing for ages. I was worried sick. Where were you?'

She didn't reply.

'Elena?'

'It doesn't matter.'

'Are you OK? Nothing's wrong, is there?'

'No.'

Elena heard her sister sigh with evident relief. 'Right. So what was that message – "he's back"? Who's back, Elena? Who?'

Fearing she might cry again, Elena kept silent.

'Elena – answer me. Who are you talking about?'

She tried to speak but struggled to find her voice in a sudden cascade of tears.

'Elena? What's happened? Who did you mean? Oh my God, you don't mean... You can't mean the American, the soldier?'

Elena screamed as she hadn't done since the war. 'Yes. Him. He came back. He came back. But now... but now...'

'Yes? What?' screeched her sister down the line. 'Tell me, Elena, just tell me.'

'But now... he's gone again.' She felt her knees weaken. Her hand with the telephone receiver dropped hitting her thigh. She felt herself gradually slide down against the wall, the words repeating themselves over and over. 'Now he's gone, now he's gone, now...' while, far away, her sister screamed her name. 'Now he's gone, now he's gone...'

Before everything went black.

*

'Elena, darling, wake up. Here, have some water.'

She managed to open her eyes, saw the blurred outline of her sister looming over her, felt the warmth inside her at the sound of her voice. She was safe now. Nina was home. Nina helped Elena to her feet and guided her through to the bedroom. Elena fell asleep as soon as she lay on the bed. When she awoke the following morning, she had no recollection of her sister undressing her, of putting her into her pyjamas. She placed her hand on her breasts, suddenly embarrassed that her sister would have seen them. But it was Nina, her lovely sister, the sister who loved her as she loved her sister. It didn't matter.

Nina brought her breakfast in bed – caffè latte and a couple of sfogliatelle. Flinging open the curtains to allow the sun in, she'd been out to the bakery, she said, and got them fresh. It was gone two in the morning by the time she arrived, she said. She'd left Roberto at his parents' place and caught a train home. She found Elena heaped on the floor, the telephone receiver hanging from the table by its cord. Nina sat on the edge of the bed, stroking Elena's arm while her sister took her breakfast. 'You don't have to tell me, you know. Not if you don't want to.'

'I don't.'

'That's fine.'

But, bit by bit, over the course of the day, Elena did tell her. Nina listened, sometimes frowning, sometimes smiling sympathetically, sometimes shaking her head, careful not to pass judgement. She knew that Elena had harboured these fantasies about the black American soldier. But she never knew the full extent of it, of how it'd become almost an obsession. She'd only been 12. The war and the bombing, the death of her parents, the disappearance and then death of her brother – it had all served to traumatise her. She remembered it too, remembered this huge man standing at the door of their bombed apartment, the first black man she'd ever seen. He was so big and looked so strong in their little, sordid home with his big voice and his presence that seemed to overshadow all else around him. Everything about him… his beauty was beyond their experience, alien almost. But she, Nina, had been no more than a spectator in the brief drama that played out between the American soldier and her sister. He had, in those few moments, shown Elena kindness. And in return, he asked for nothing. Nothing. And for a little girl, traumatised by the cruelty of war, his kindness was almost unfathomable; it had seared her. After he'd gone, they both remained still, staring at the space he had, all too briefly, occupied. It felt as if they'd been visited by an angel and his presence and departure had left them speechless. Reflecting on it later, Nina felt that, in some ways, Elena had been traumatised again – if there can be such a thing as traumatised by kindness. A beacon of light in the hell that was Naples in 1944. It had showed them both, but especially Elena, that even in war, even when everything you know and hold dear has been ripped away from you, there is sometimes, occasionally, kindness in the world. But life moves on; Nina had moved on. Yet Elena, little Elena, hadn't. Nina hadn't realised until now, eleven years later, just how much her sister had been affected that day. In some ways, the incident had infantilised her. Her body grew and developed, as did her mind – but not to the extent it should have. Part of her mind had never left that day in April 1944 and her heart seemed totally given to the angel who momentarily had appeared before them in their darkest hour.

'The baby's due in November.'

'Is it?' It was now coming up to lunch. Nina was feeling distinctly hungry but Elena, now stretched out on the living room settee, had begun talking and Nina knew she had to stay and listen, however long it took. 'Is it their first?'

Elena shrugged her shoulders. 'I don't know.'

Sitting on the floor next to the settee, Nina rubbed Elena's arm. 'He's right, you know, your American. About living for tomorrow.'

'I'm busy tomorrow. Swimming.'

'Elena, what he means...' Her sister winked at her. She knew what she meant. 'Come on, up you get, lazy bones, you can cut up some tomatoes for me.'

Together, they prepared enough food for lunch and dinner, talking and singing along to songs on the radio.

'Don't you want to go back to Roberto?'

'I rang him earlier. He's fine. He understands. Oh, and he sends his love.'

Elena stopped. 'Does he?'

'Of course. He's very fond of you, you know.'

'That's nice. Are you going to marry him?'

'One day. Maybe. I just need to work out if it's me he loves or my book royalties.'

'Really?'

'No, I'm only joking. It's me he loves,' she cried in a sing-song voice, twirling around the kitchen with an invisible dance partner. 'Me and only me!'

Elena, chopping knife in hand, laughed.

Such was the volume of the radio and their boisterousness, that it took a while before they heard the knock on their apartment door.

Elena's mouth went dry with fear. Surely, she thought, he hadn't come to find her. He had, after all, written down her address. 'Who could that be?' she said.

Nina, catching the apprehension in her sister's voice, suddenly felt the same. She didn't want him here, raising Elena's hopes.

'How did he get up here?' asked Elena.

'Someone must have held the door open for him downstairs.' Nina went to the door. She wished she'd had one of those spyholes in her door like she'd seen in some American films. If it was him, the American, she'd push him away. Big man or no big man, she wasn't prepared to allow him near her sister; it'd be too much for her.

She opened the door but a fraction. Standing on the landing beneath the passageway light was not a large black American but a small, fidgety local boy, about 20 years old, a sweep of jet-black hair, wearing little more than a vest and a pair of shorts. Her relief did not squash her irritation. 'Yes, what is it?'

'Is Elena in, please?'

'Who are you?'

'I'm Antonio. I–'

'Who?'

'Antonio. I – I work at the p-pool. The – the swimming pool.' Nina noticed he was holding something out. 'It's Elena's swimming cap.'

'Is it? You'd better come in.'

It was only when he came into the full light of the apartment, she realised what an Adonis this boy was, lean and muscly. So even more incongruous that he should be so shy and unsure of himself. But where was Elena? Nina called her sister's name out. 'She was here a minute ago,' she said.

'I c-could just leave it with you, if you like,' he said, twisting the swimming cap in his hands.

'She'll be in her…'

The bedroom door opened and Elena emerged in a pink skirt and a fetching blouse. 'Have you…' The "don't say it" expression on Elena's face stopped Nina from finishing the sentence.

'Oh, hello, Antonio.'

'Hi, I – you look nice.'

'Well, thank you,' said Elena in a *I know I do* type of voice.

'I called yesterday but you were out. I just wanted to bring your cap back. You forgot it – yesterday.'

'Did I? Silly me,' she said, subconsciously flicking back her hair. 'That's very kind of you.' Narrowing her eyes, she asked, 'How did you know where I live?'

'You're a member, aren't you? So… so I looked up your membership card in the file at work. You… you don't mind, d-do you?'

'No, it's all right. Do you want a lemonade?'

'Well…' Antonio glanced at Nina.

'I'll get you one,' said Nina, happy to escape to the kitchen.

Having served up two ice-cold lemonades, Nina slipped back to the kitchen, a wry smile on her face. Best leave them to it, she thought. After all, who knows where it might lead?

December 1955

'Elena? Elena, the post has come. Something for you.'

Elena emerged from the bathroom in her dressing gown, her hair wrapped up in a coiled towel. Nina passed her a brown paper package. 'For me?'

'Look at the postmark.'

Her heartbeat quickened on seeing the American Christmas stamp and the New Jersey postmark. 'Oh, Lordy, he's sent me a present. I've not even sent a card.'

'You don't know his address, silly.'

Hoping her sister wouldn't mind, Elena took the package to her bedroom; she needed to be alone. Unwrapping the brown paper, she found a card and a rectangular-shaped box wrapped in Christmas paper. She smiled at the jolly snowman on the card. Opening it, a black and white photo fell out. It was of a tiny, sleeping, contented-looking baby wrapped in a white lace shawl. Inside Brad had written a note but it was English. She'd read it later, she thought, perhaps with Nina's help. Unwrapping the present, her heart skipped on seeing the familiar leather case. Unlocking the little hook, she opened and there was Brad's watch. She squealed with delight. Inside the case was a little note. "With love from Brad. X". 'Wonderful,' she muttered to herself. The watch had stopped. Winding it up, it began ticking. What a relief. She changed the hands to show the correct time. She was pleased to see that Brad hadn't changed the glass – it was still cracked.

She heard Nina's voice. 'You alright in there?'

'Come in, come in.'

She showed her sister the photo.

'Isn't she adorable?' said Nina.

'And look, he's returned the watch.'

Nina took her hand. 'Have you read the note?'

'Can you help me?'

Together, they deciphered Brad's handwriting and, with the help of a dictionary, managed to read his note inside the card…

Dear Elena,

I hope this finds you well. We are knee-deep in snow here in New Jersey.

As you can see, we've had a baby – a girl. She was born November 12. Mother and child are doing well.

I wish you (and your sister) a Merry Christmas and I wish you a happy 1956.

Lots of love,

Brad.

PS Hope you don't mind but we've called the baby Elena Grace.

'Oh, Elena, how lovely. Elena Grace. You must be pleased.'

Elena would have answered, would have said yes if she hadn't been crying so much.

October 1956

It was to be a small wedding, just a handful of guests. Neither Elena nor Antonio had many friends and, sadly, neither had much in the way of family now.

Elena stood at the end of the aisle near the chapel entrance, butterflies in her stomach. Behind her, Nina, her maid of honour, and beside her, Antonio's father, who had agreed to give her away. The autumnal sun shone through the stained-glass windows, leaving colourful patterns on the flagstones. She could see Antonio in his morning suit waiting for her with his best man next to the altar chatting to the priest. An organ played quietly in the background. She loved her dress – Nina had helped choose it and had paid for it. The swishy skirt, which reached just below her knees, was made of silk with a satin underskirt, and the bodice made from Chantilly lace. A pink sash pinned with a brooch acted as a belt. If only her mother could see her now. In her hand, a small bouquet of purple pansies.

Things had turned out well. Some people expressed surprise at how quickly she and Antonio were getting married. They'd only been courting a few months. But Elena knew it felt right. She loved him in a way she never would have thought possible. In the year they'd been together they had not had a single cross word. And they were Italian; they were meant to argue! Actually, there was the one time but she preferred to gloss over that. After all, Antonio had been acting out the goodness of his heart. One day, a few weeks ago, he had borrowed Brad's watch and taken it to a jeweller to get the glass replaced. He presented it to her, anticipating gratitude and appreciation for his thoughtfulness. How mistaken he was! Unable to stem her fury, Elena shrieked, cried and thumped him. How dare he? How could he have been so stupid? The crack had been part of the watch's identity, part of its history. He had no right. It took her a whole day to calm down. She'd sent Brad, Minnie and baby Elena an invitation but, as expected, received a reply thanking her but regretting they would be unable to attend. The wedding and her love of Antonio had occupied her mind these last few months; she thought only occasionally of Brad now, and for that she was thankful. But she knew, would always know, that Brad had, in some ways, saved her – not once but twice. First in 1944 and again last year. If she hadn't seen him, if he hadn't talked to her in that hotel that Saturday night, she would have remained a twelve-year-old girl trapped in the body of a 23-year-old woman. He had released her, allowed her to grow up, to become a woman, soon to be a married woman. And for that, she'd always be grateful.

Nina placed her hand on her shoulder. 'You OK, sister?'

Elena nodded despite feeling almost sick with nerves. 'Never happier.'

Antonio's father smiled at her. 'You look gorgeous, my dear. My son is a lucky man.'

'Thank you, sir.'

'Please, call me Paolo. I'm about to be your father-in-law after all.' She liked the name Paolo. It was her brother's name. The organ music stopped, conversations came to an abrupt halt. 'Ah, I think we're ready.' He offered his arm. 'May I?' he asked.

Feeling weak with nerves yet unable to stop grinning, Elena looped her arm through his.

'Are we ready?' he asked.

'Yes, I'm ready,' she said, taking a deep breath.

The organ restarted, the opening chords of Handel's Messiah blasting out across the chapel. 'Oh, blow me,' said Paolo, suddenly looking worried. 'I've just realised. I've... I've forgotten something.' He glanced back at Nina. 'I'm very sorry. I won't be a moment.'

And with that, he ran out of the chapel, leaving Elena feeling very alone and vulnerable. 'Where's he gone?' she asked.

'I don't know,' said Nina, her face creased with concern. 'The priest doesn't look too happy.'

Turning, Elena saw the priest shrugging his shoulders, his eyebrows raised. 'Lordy, I don't like this,' she muttered, gripping her bouquet of pansies. 'Where's he gone? What's he doing?'

It took a moment or two before she was aware of someone standing next to her, a shadow falling over her. 'May I have the honour?' said the familiar voice.

The tears came in an instant, her mouth gaped open trying to speak but no sound emerged, her voice seized by the pounding of her heart.

'Don't you look a picture? You look one hundred per cent beautiful, Missy.'

'Brad… you – you c-came.'

'Why, of course. Did you really think I would miss this? Come, Missy, stop your crying now; your make-up will run, and, what's more, you're making this old negro cry too.'

'I'm sorry.'

'Don't apologise now; it's good to shed a tear of happiness. But we have to start walking now, you and me. I

can see a handsome young man waiting, and, Miss… I reckon
he's waiting for you.'

THE END

Novels by Rupert Colley:

The Love and War Series
Song of Sorrow
The Lost Daughter
The White Venus
The Woman on the Train
The Black Maria
My Brother the Enemy
Anastasia
The Mist Before Our Eyes
The Darkness We Leave Behind

The Searight Saga
This Time Tomorrow
The Unforgiving Sea
The Red Oak

Rupertcolley.com